Editors: Ann Redpath, Etienne Delessert
Art Director: Rita Marshall
Publisher: George R. Peterson, Jr.

Copyright © 1984 Creative Education, Inc., 123 S. Broad Street,
Mankato, Minnesota 56001, USA. American Edition.
Copyright © 1984 Grasset & Fasquelle, Paris – Editions 24 Heures, Lausanne. French Edition.
International copyrights reserved in all countries.

Library of Congress Catalog Card No.: 83-71183
Grimm, Jakob and Wilhelm; Rapunzel
Mankato, MN: Creative Education, Inc.; 32 pages. ISBN: 0-87191-936-2

Printed in Switzerland by Imprimeries Réunies S.A. Lausanne.

RAPUNZEL

JAKOB & WILHELM GRIMM
illustrated by
MICHAEL HAGUE

CREATIVE EDUCATION INC.

ONCE UPON A TIME

THERE lived a man and his wife who were very unhappy because they had no children. These good people had a little window at the back of their house, which looked into the most lovely garden, full of all kinds of beautiful flowers and vegetables; but the garden was surrounded by a high wall, and no one dared to enter it, for it belonged to a witch of great power, who was feared by the whole world. One day the woman stood at the window overlooking the garden, and saw there a bed full of the finest rampion. The leaves looked so fresh and green that she longed to eat them. The desire grew day by day, and just because she knew she couldn't possibly get any, she pined away and became quite pale and wretched. Then her husband grew alarmed and said:

"What ails you, dear wife?"

"Oh," she answered, "if I don't get some rampion to eat out of the garden behind the house, I know I shall die."

The man, who loved her dearly, thought to himself, "Come! rather than let your wife die you shall fetch her some rampion, no matter the cost." So at dusk he climbed over the wall into the witch's garden, and, hastily gathering a handful of rampion leaves, he returned with them to his wife. She made them into a salad, which tasted so good that her longing for the forbidden food was greater than ever. If she were to know any peace of mind, her husband should climb over the garden wall again, and fetch her some more. So at dusk, over he went. But when he reached the other side, he drew back in terror, for there, standing before him, was the old witch.

"How dare you," she said, with a wrathful glance, "climb into my garden and steal my rampion like a common thief? You shall suffer for your foolhardiness."

"Oh!" he implored, "pardon my presumption; necessity alone drove me to the deed. My wife saw your rampion from her window, and conceived such a desire for it that she would certainly have died if her wish had not been gratified." Then the Witch's anger was a little appeased, and she said:

"If it's as you say, you may take as much rampion away with you as you like, but on one condition only—that you give me the child your wife will shortly bring into the world. All shall go well with it, and I will look after it like a mother."

The man in his terror agreed to everything she asked, and as soon as the child was born the Witch appeared, and having given it the name of Rapunzel, which is the same as rampion, she carried it off with her.

Rapunzel was the most beautiful child under the sun. When she was twelve years old the Witch shut her up in a tower, in the middle of a great wood, and the tower had neither stairs nor doors, only a small window, high up at the very top. When the old Witch wanted to get in, she stood underneath and called out:

"Rapunzel, Rapunzel,
Let down your golden hair,"

for Rapunzel had wonderful long hair, and it was as fine as spun gold. Whenever she heard the Witch's voice she unloosed her braids, and let her hair fall down out of the window about twenty yards below, and the old Witch climbed up by it.

After they had lived like this for a few years, it happened one day that a Prince was riding through the wood and passed by the tower. As he drew near it he heard someone singing so sweetly that he stood still spell-bound, and listened. It was Rapunzel in her loneliness, trying to while away the time by letting her sweet voice ring out into the wood. The Prince longed to see the owner of the voice, but he sought in vain for a door in the tower. He rode home, but he was so haunted by the song he had heard that he returned every day to the wood and listened.

One day, when he was standing thus behind a tree, he saw the old Witch approach and heard her call out:

"Rapunzel, Rapunzel,
Let down your golden hair."

Then Rapunzel let down her braids, and the Witch climbed up by them.

"So that's the staircase, is it?" said the Prince. "Then I too will climb it and try my luck."

So on the following day, at dusk, he went to the foot of the tower and cried:

"Rapunzel, Rapunzel,
Let down your golden hair,"

and as soon as she had let it down the Prince climbed up.

At first Rapunzel was terribly frightened when a man came in, for she had never seen one before; but the Prince spoke to her so kindly, and told her at once that his heart had been so touched by her singing, that he felt he should know no peace of mind till he had seen her. Very soon Rapunzel forgot her fear, and when he asked her to marry him, she consented at once. "For," she thought, "he is young and handsome, and I'll certainly be happier with him than with the old Witch." So she put her hand in his and said:

"Yes, I will gladly go with you, only how am I to get down out of the tower? Every time you come to see me you must bring a skein of silk with you, and I will make a ladder of them, and when it is finished I will climb down by it, and you will take me away on your horse."

They arranged that, till the ladder was ready, he was to come to her every evening, because the old woman was with her during the day.

The old Witch, of course, knew nothing of what was going on, till one day Rapunzel, not thinking of what she was about, turned to the Witch and said:

"How is it, good mother, that you are so much harder to pull up than the young Prince? He is always with me in a moment."

"Oh! you wicked child," cried the Witch. "What is this I hear? I thought I had hidden you safely from the whole world, and in spite of it you have managed to deceive me."

In her wrath she seized Rapunzel's beautiful hair, wound it round and round her left hand, and then grasping a pair of scissors in her right, snip snap, off it came, and the beautiful braids lay on the ground. And, worse than this, she was so hard-hearted that she took Rapunzel to a lonely desert place, and there left her to live in loneliness and misery.

But on the evening of the day in which she had driven poor Rapunzel away, the Witch fastened the braids on to a hook in the window, and when the Prince came and called out:

"Rapunzel, Rapunzel,
Let down your golden hair."

She let them down, and the Prince climbed up as usual, but instead of his beloved Rapunzel, he found the old Witch, who fixed her evil, glittering eyes on him, and cried mockingly:

"Ah, ah! you thought to find your lady love, but the pretty bird has flown and its song is dumb; that cat caught it, and will scratch out your eyes too. Rapunzel is lost to you for ever —you will never see her more."

The Prince was beside himself with grief, and in his despair he jumped right down from the tower, and, though he escaped with his life, the thorns among which he fell pierced his eyes out.

Then he wandered, blind,
and miserable, through the
wood, eating nothing but
roots and berries, and weep-
ing and lamenting the loss of
his lovely bride. So he wandered about for some years, as
wretched and unhappy as he
could well be, and at last he
came to the desert place where
Rapunzel was living.

Suddenly he heard a voice which seemed strangely famil-iar to him. He walked eagerly in the direction of the sound, and when he was quite close, Rapunzel recognized him and fell on his neck and wept. But two of her tears touched his eyes, and in a moment they became quite clear again, and he saw as well as he ever had. Then he led her to his kingdom, where they were received and welcomed with great joy, and they lived happily ever after.

398.2   12186
Gr

Grimm Brothers

Rapunzel

	DATE DUE		
Preston	FEB 25	Miller	
DEC 9		Rodz.	
DEC 2 0	MAR 13	APR 8	
MAR 1 0	MAR 25	Campbell	
APR 8	APR 1 5	APR 26	
SEP 1 8	APR 8		
OCT 2 4	NOV 1 2		
OCT 2 2	FEB 1 7		
NOV 5	MAR 2 4		
NOV 1 2	MAY 5		
FEB 9	SEP 2 9		